Kalibal:

A Poetic Tale

Leon X

Poetic Tale:

Meet Kalibal. Kalibal runs his own covenant on the etches of society with his servants and servants alone. No outsiders. His ways of life are differed than those deemed "normal" in society. The biggest change? The cooking and roasting of human flesh to a supreme delicacy unseen in the world.

Kalibal also known as the Chef of Chefs and the Butcher of Butchers knows his duty. While under the famous Full Moon of the Blue, he takes advantage of the special full moon day to its fullest. He orders families to be cooked to the highest order and is ready to feast upon them with elements of secret spices and paste to add flavor to his deific tongue.

The real question is, is Kalibal and his covenant even human to begin with?

"Humans, Humans, Humans..."

– Leon X

Covenant Leader Kalibal

<u>1</u>
Feed them to Thy,
Are they not going to be'th with Thy forever?
Am Thy not the finest Chef?

<u>2</u>
Of all cultures and of creeds?
Am Thy not using humans?
Thus,

<u>3</u>

Am Thy not of the universal?

Are not these beings going to Hell anyway?

Even the people within a constructed society by a genius

whom thinketh they are of good?

<u>4</u>

Am Thy not to feast till Thy stomach is of full?
Is this not a way?
Am Thy not an expression?!

<u>**5**</u>

Of God and or else whom?
That does not matter as of now,
Enough of tis speech unto morals,

<u>6</u>
Feed me tis family,
And then another family under the Full of Moon,
And then Thy enemies for the friends of thine whom also
need'th flesh of the human,

<u>**7**</u>

Pathetic beings of flesh,
When the demons cometh and taketh over for twelve
years,
They will only be'th of flesh and of bone,

<u>**8**</u>
Used in necromantic rituals,
And darker rituals unseen for mortal eyes,
For the summon'ing,

<u>9</u>
And the excess of bodies use'd for intergalactic space
travel through the dark spaces between,
Only the few will be of chosen,
And of their kin,

<u>**10**</u>
And kin a'lone,
Direct family a'lone,
And a'lone,

<u>11</u>

It shall be'th,
Am Thy not of all races?
Are they not of Thy feast?

<u>**12**</u>
Is it that,
Thy will'th drinketh their blood as of wine after flesh is of
consume'd?
Then it must'th be,

<u>13</u>
Of all cultures so it is to be'th,
Is not around the world the taste of different?
Am Thy not a God?

<u>**14**</u>
Or am Thy of the Horned?
Is it not Thy?
The Lord?

<u>15</u>

It is not?
Am Thy not of this world?
And is not this world of Thy?

<u>16</u>
FEED ME!
THAT FAMILY,
AND FAMILY A'LONE!

<u>17</u>

UNDER THE MOON OF FULL AND FULL MOON
A'LONE,
THEIR BODIES WILL BE'TH FOOD FOR
MONTHS UPON END,
AM THY NOT THE FINEST BUTCHER OF
HUMAN FLESH AND FLESH A'LONE?!

<u>**18**</u>

Am Thy not the Chef of Chefs?
The Butcher of Butchers?
Are not the hamstrings of the finest?

<u>**19**</u>

And of the finest a'lone?
Or is it of the biceps attached to bone dipped into spice
before the cook'd?
Or of the trapezius and pectoralis dipped into paste of the
spices after the cook'd?

<u>**20**</u>

Yet the holy tongue is a delicacy reserved for the few...
Thy am to wonder as of now this new ideation of spices
and of pastes,
As Thy hath truly forgot'th the power of spices and of
pastes,

<u>21</u>

O'UUUUUUUUUU!

Excitement rushes Thy arteries and of veins!

Thy must rest'th...

<u>**22**</u>
And rest'th a'lone,
Yet Thy ponder...
What is of this?

<u>23</u>

Is not the devouring of man maketh Thy a man?!
Is not the devouring of child maketh Thy a child?!
Is not devouring of woman maketh Thy a woman?!

<u>24</u>

Cauldrons of bodies to be of cook'd!
Three cauldrons!
Five bodies within a cauldron of three!

<u>**25**</u>
Ah!
Am Thy not the finest craftsman of Chefmanship?
Of the Fine Art of Butchery?!

<u>**26**</u>
Bonemanship?!
Envied by both the Hells and of the Heavens,
Am Thy not the Son of Whom?

<u>**27**</u>
God?
Or of the Horned?
HAHAHA!

<u>**28**</u>

Thou are not to knoweth!
Am Thy not the Creator of Higher Beings?
Thus are they not Thy Creation?

<u>29</u>

As meals to eat'th?
Do not all souls returneth to Thy and Thy a'lone?
Bow down when thou see'th of Thy and hear'th of Thy
presence a'lone,

<u>30</u>

Mortals whom Thy will eat'th with only bone to be of left,
And marrow to be used for more pastes of vitality,
Time for a'nother rest...

<u>**31**</u>
Servants!
Worketh on these mortals,
Five bodies per cauldron as of be'fore,

<u>**32**</u>
Or if feeling of roast onto the roast'd'bed,
And maketh no mistake,
Hairs off,

<u>33</u>

Skin off and cast a'side beautifully...
No gluteus maximus unless thou are to wisheth for thou
own sake,
Five cook'd within each cauldron as Thy hath order'd,

<u>**34**</u>

And for those mortals with strong abdominal muscle and
of obliques,
Craft and cook with spice over the soothing roast,
Do not forget'th the latissimus dorsi as with the trapezius,

<u>35</u>

Keep'th frozen till Thy am to speak of it,

And finally...

The finest cook'd muscle with the most chomp,

<u>36</u>
Sternocleidomastoid muscles of the two,
Fine roasted,
With paste of barbeque or of honey and of spices all of
o'ver,

<u>37</u>

Thy am to rest'th once more a'now,
Do not maketh a mistake!
Understand'th this servants...

<u>**38**</u>
Do not maketh a mistake!
Am Thy not of perfection?
Are not Thy works of epicurean perfection?!

<u>**39**</u>

And now Thy am to knoweth,

That greatness is only within,

Not without...

<u>**40**</u>
Thy am to rest'th...
The closing of eyes is of need'd,
Till' the changing of color in sky to dark'th,

<u>**41**</u>

Rest is of complete'th...
The time hath cometh,
Under the Moon of the Fullest and of Finest Glow,

<u>**42**</u>

Is it not of a Man?
Or of a Woman?
It must be'th of a Moon of Womanly!

<u>**43**</u>

As a woman whom hath menstruated as there be of a
Blood Moon?
Enough of this speak of the Moon,
Tis smell...

<u>44</u>

The cook'd smell...
These mortal bodies are of the finest...
But Thy will'th not cook'th nor eat'th the vaginal or of the
ovaries,

$$\underline{45}$$

Nor of the male's anatomy of such region,
Is it not known it is of the cursed?
So Thy am to knoweth...

<u>46</u>
Yet,
Do Thy not wish'th to eat'th thine enemies?
Thy shall not think of such ignorant flesh to be of
consume'd,

<u>47</u>

Thy shall let'th the raptors of alli eat'th them as raw flesh
without the cook,
Are not of the raptors Thy kin and kin a'lone?
Enough of tis',

<u>48</u>

Should not the finest Chef be of need'th to eat'th and
eat'th and rest'th a'lone?
The mi'nute rest'th wunce a'more be'th of complete...
Sleep'th is only for the weak,

<u>**49**</u>

Servants! It is time!
Poureth the blood into the chalices,
And of the chalices of gold a'lone,

<u>**50**</u>
And eat'th up!
The greatest taste!
With colorful paste and of spices unknowest to man,

<u>51</u>
Is it not of man and woman a'lone,
Or of child that be of the finest flesh when of cook'd?
Such young flesh of bone and of muscle,

<u>**52**</u>

Never touched by life as of yet,
Purity in meat to be of consume'd,
And mi'nute flesh and of small bone a'lone,

<u>53</u>
Thy am only doing what is of needed,
Am Thy not decomposing for the Earth and Earth
a'lone?
Under the Full of Moon over this bless'd night sky
without clouds of obstruction,

<u>54</u>

Thy God is of pleased,
Or is it of the Horned?
Are they not of the same?

Or is One greater than the Other?
Did not One create'th the Other?
Or am Thy of folly?

<u>**56**</u>
Is not to eat,
Divine?
Then why not eat'th all?

<u>57</u>

Is not Creation of the Divine?
HAHAHA!
So they say'th...

<u>**58**</u>

So why not eat'th?
Why not eat'th the world if possible?
And cook'th its flesh for Thy and only Thy and Thy
servants to consumeth?

<u>**59**</u>

Thy will sticketh to humans and humans a'lone,
Is not Hell only a word?
And Heaven only an experience?

<u>**60**</u>
Servants!
Fill tis' chalice of gold with a'more blood of mortals,
Of the infant tis' time!

<u>**61**</u>

Thy am of need'th of youth!
O' thank you kind sir!
The freshest blood is always of the young...

<u>62</u>

The feast,
Reserved for only kings,
And of queens,

<u>63</u>

Am Thy not of royal and royalty a'lone whom the Gods
and the Devil envy?
Is it not thine enemies whom are truly to be of eat'th?
And of course,

<u>64</u>

Rivals a'lone?

O!

Forgot'th!

<u>65</u>

They will'th be of fed to Thy gators of alli,
And they a'lone...
For why would a Creation liketh Thyself,

<u>66</u>

Eat'th thine enemies and rivals,
Whom wished badly and death upon Thy?
Enough of this...

<u>67</u>

Servant! More rib of man!
The space in'between each is of the finest,
Did not God createth woman out of man?

<u>**68**</u>
Servant!
More rib of a woman now!
Let thy taste'th the difference...

<u>69</u>

A balance in fleshly tastes,
O' what fine cuisine of the Earth and of Earth a'lone,
Yet what sleep'th is to be of caused by such cook'd flesh...

<u>**70**</u>

Thy must rest'th wunce a'more,
And rest'th a'lone,
Till' the next Moon of Full,

<u>**71**</u>
May it be of the Blood,
Yet...
Thy must containeth Thyself,

<u>**72**</u>

Unless Thy and Thy servants are of extreme hunger
wunce more,
The Moon of A'new willeth always bringeth change,
Unto man, woman and of child?

<u>**73**</u>

Did not God create'th such changes of the Moon?
Did He not create'th mastication and of taste?
Of all flesh and of flesh a'lone?

<u>74</u>
Of Man?
Woman?
And of Child?

<u>**75**</u>

Thus...

Am Thy not of God?

And to eat'th flesh that is of He and He a'lone?

<u>76</u>
Am Thy not of a Higher Be'ing?
Is it not to eat'th of humanly flesh,
To be of the superior?

End.

About the Author

Leon X is a novelist and poet.

Visit www.leonxtheauthor.com for more information on the author.

Thank you for supporting.